P9-DGV-406

A Note from Michelle about My Fourth-Grade Mess

Hi! I'm Michelle Tanner. I'm nine years old. And I'm in big trouble!

My teacher says I cheated on my math test. I didn't cheat—I would never cheat! I've been working extra hard on my math lately. My whole family has been helping me out—and that means a lot of help. Because I have a lot of family.

There's my dad and my two older sisters, D. J. and Stephanie. But that's not all.

My mom died when I was little. So my uncle Jesse moved in to help Dad take care of us. So did Joey Gladstone. He's my dad's friend from college. It's almost like having three dads. But that's still not all!

First Uncle Jesse got married to Becky Donaldson. Then they had twin boys, Nicky and Alex. The twins are four years old now. And they're so cute.

That's nine people. Our dog, Comet, makes ten. Sure, it gets kind of crazy sometimes. But I wouldn't change it for anything. It's so much fun to live in a full house!

FULL HOUSE™ MICHELLE novels

The Great Pet Project
The Super-Duper Sleepover Party
My Two Best Friends
Lucky, Lucky Day
The Ghost in My Closet
Ballet Surprise
Major League Trouble
My Fourth-Grade Mess

Available from MINSTREL Books

For orders other than by individual consumers, Pocket Books grants a discount on the purchase of **10 or more** copies of single titles for special markets or premium use. For further details, please write to the Vice-President of Special Markets, Pocket Books, 1633 Broadway, New York, NY 10019-6785, 8th Floor.

For information on how individual consumers can place orders, please write to Mail Order Department, Simon & Schuster Inc., 200 Old Tappan Road, Old Tappan, NJ 07675.

FULL HOUSE™
Michelle

My Fourth-Grade Mess

Cathy East Dubowski

A Parachute Press Book

Published by POCKET BOOKS
New York   London   Toronto   Sydney   Tokyo   Singapore

The sale of this book without its cover is unauthorized. If you purchased this book without a cover, you should be aware that it was reported to the publisher as "unsold and destroyed." Neither the author nor the publisher has received payment for the sale of this "stripped book."

This book is a work of fiction. Names, characters, places and incidents are products of the author's imagination or are used fictitiously. Any resemblance to actual events or locales or persons, living or dead, is entirely coincidental.

A MINSTREL PAPERBACK *Original*

A Minstrel Book published by
POCKET BOOKS, a division of Simon & Schuster Inc.
1230 Avenue of the Americas, New York, NY 10020

A PARACHUTE PRESS BOOK

READING Copyright © and ™ 1996 by Warner Bros.

FULL HOUSE, characters, names and all related indicia are trademarks of Warner Bros. © 1996.

All rights reserved, including the right to reproduce this book or portions thereof in any form whatsoever. For information address Pocket Books, 1230 Avenue of the Americas, New York, NY 10020

ISBN: 0-671-53576-5

First Minstrel Books printing May 1996

10 9 8 7 6 5 4 3 2 1

A MINSTREL BOOK and colophon are registered trademarks of Simon & Schuster Inc.

Cover photo by Schultz Photography

Printed in the U.S.A.

My Fourth-Grade Mess

Chapter 1

♥ "Hey, Michelle!"

Nine-year-old Michelle Tanner felt a tiny tug on her strawberry blond ponytail. She slammed her math book closed and whirled around.

Jeff Farrington grinned at her. He was sitting right behind her on the school bus. Jeff had light brown hair and big, dark brown eyes. He was always kidding around.

"Are you ready for our math test?" Jeff asked.

"Ugh—math!" Michelle groaned.

Their fourth-grade teacher, Mrs. Yoshida, had planned a big math test for today. Math was *not* Michelle's best subject. She was a little nervous about the test.

"Do we *have* to talk about it?" Michelle asked. "It makes my head hurt."

"It makes my head hurt too," Jeff said. "Maybe we should put our heads together," he added.

"I guess so," Michelle said. "Two heads are better than one—right?"

She had heard her dad say that. It meant that two people thinking together could solve a problem better than one person alone.

"When are two heads *not* better than one?" Jeff asked.

"I don't know," Michelle answered. "When?"

"When they're on the same body," Jeff

joked. "Because then you have to pay double for haircuts!"

Michelle giggled. Jeff was *so* funny. And he was always smiling and in a good mood.

That's why I like him, Michelle thought. That's why *everybody* likes him. Jeff was the most popular guy in the fourth grade.

"Why are people with two heads never lonely?" Jeff asked.

Michelle shrugged.

"Because they always have somebody to talk to!" Jeff replied.

Michelle laughed.

Jeff moved into the empty seat beside her. "Michelle, can you do me a big, big favor?" he asked.

"Sure," Michelle answered.

Was he being serious? she wondered. Or getting ready to crack another joke?

Jeff looked down at his open notebook. "Well, I had to babysit my little brothers

3

last night. Do you know how that is?" he asked.

Michelle rolled her eyes. "Do I ever! I have twin cousins named Nicky and Alex. Sometimes I have to help look after them. They're only four, and they're really cute. But sometimes they drive me crazy!"

Jeff chuckled. "My brothers made me crazy last night. I couldn't even finish my math homework. So, do you think I could take a peek at yours before we get to school?"

"Are you kidding?" Michelle said. "I'm not that great at math."

"Me neither," Jeff said. "I think I'm allergic to it!" He pretended to sneeze.

"Maybe that's my problem too!" Michelle sneezed also.

Jeff grinned at her. "But you are doing better in math than I am. Please, Michelle? Just a quick peek," he said.

"Well, okay," Michelle said. "I guess I could help you figure out the problems."

She unzipped her pink-and-blue backpack. She pulled out her notebook and opened it to her math homework.

"Which ones do you need help with?" she asked.

Jeff gave a nervous laugh. "We're only a couple of blocks from school," he said. "There's no time for a math lesson. Just let me look at your paper."

"Uh, well . . ."

"Please please please *pleeeeease?*" Jeff yanked off his red baseball cap and held it to his chest. He stared at her and pretended he was about to cry.

Michelle shook her head. "Okay, *okay!* You look like my dog, Comet, when he's begging for treats!" She handed Jeff her notebook.

"Thanks, Michelle!" Jeff said. "You're a real pal!"

Michelle grinned. It felt cool to have the most popular guy in the fourth grade call you his pal. "No problem," she said. "What are friends for?"

But then she noticed that Jeff was taking out a blank sheet of paper.

Hey! Michelle thought. Jeff didn't have trouble *finishing* his homework. He never even started it!

And now he was copying all of the problems—and all of her answers.

Oh, well, she told herself. I guess it's all right. I mean, we're pals.

Jeff would do the same for me—right?

Chapter

2

♥ Pencils are a pain! Michelle thought.

It was later that morning. Michelle was in the middle of the math test. She flipped her pencil over and began to erase another problem. Her paper was getting messy from so much erasing. "Yuck," Michelle muttered.

Mrs. Yoshida stopped by Michelle's desk. She put a finger to her lips. "No talking, Michelle." Her voice was kind, but firm.

"Ooops! Sorry," Michelle whispered.

Fractions made her so mad!

Michelle's math grades had not been so good this year. But she had been working extra hard lately.

Her dad had been helping her. So had everyone else in the Tanner household. Even Comet, the dog, helped her out. He let Michelle hug him when she felt like giving up.

Michelle felt like she could use a hug right now!

Why can't we use calculators or computers to do math? Michelle wondered. That's what grown-ups do.

Cashiers in the grocery store don't add up the groceries with a pencil and paper. They use that beeping computer thing.

And her father uses his computer to pay the bills. She had even seen him use a calculator when he cooked. He would double the amount of food in his recipes. He did that a lot because there were so many people to feed in their house.

There was Michelle and her dad, Danny Tanner.

Then there were Michelle's two older sisters. Stephanie was in eighth grade. And D.J. was in college. That was four people.

There were also Uncle Jesse and his wife, Becky. And their twin boys, Alex and Nicky. That was four more. Four plus four was eight.

And then there was Joey Gladstone. Joey was her dad's best friend. He had moved in to help when Michelle's mother died. That was back when she was a baby. Now Joey was part of the family. Eight plus one was nine. And Comet, their golden retriever, made ten.

Adding up a family was easy. But adding up fractions was driving Michelle crazy!

Michelle squirmed in her seat. I'm going

to blow this test, she thought. I just know it!

She glanced up. Uh-oh. Mrs. Yoshida was watching her.

Then Michelle remembered what her father had told her that morning. "If you run into trouble on your test—stop. Take a deep breath. Think of something pleasant. Then go back to work.

"And remember, Michelle. If you knew everything already, you wouldn't need to go to school. Just do your best. That's all that matters to me." He gave her a big hug. "Of course, it's nice if you keep your columns neat, too."

That was her father—he liked *everything* neat!

"Okay, Dad, here goes!" Michelle put down her pencil and stopped, just like he said. She took a deep breath.

What was next?

Oh, yeah. Think of something pleasant. Michelle glanced around the room.

I know! she thought. The *end* of the math test!

Michelle giggled. Hey! It worked! She really *did* feel better. She picked up her pencil again.

Look out, math test. Here I come! she thought.

She took the rest of the problems one by one. She tried to keep her numbers neat and her columns straight. Being neat really did help. At last she was finished.

Next step: Double check each problem. That was Aunt Becky's idea.

Aha! Michelle thought. Problem number four. That should be a seven instead of an eight. Good save, Michelle! she told herself. She quickly fixed the answer.

Suddenly Michelle got a funny feeling. As if someone was watching her.

She looked up at Mrs. Yoshida. Nope.

The teacher was writing in her lesson book.

Michelle glanced at the row of desks across from hers. That's where Jeff Farrington sat. He jerked a little, as if she had caught him watching her.

Had Jeff been staring at her paper?

Michelle squinted. Jeff saw her and made a funny face. Then he sniffed his paper—and sneezed! He was allergic to math, all right!

Michelle held her nose to keep from laughing out loud. It made her breath come out in little snorts.

Jeff grinned and went back to working on his test.

Up front, Mrs. Yoshida cleared her throat and glared at Michelle.

Michelle ducked her head and stared down at her paper.

I guess Jeff wasn't peeking at my paper, she thought. He was probably just taking a break, like Dad told me to do. Michelle went back to checking her problems. She decided to clean up her paper a little more, too.

But a few minutes later Michelle got a creepy feeling again—as if tiny porcupines were dancing up her spine.

This time she didn't move her head. She peeked out the corner of her eye.

Jeff's elbow was propped on his desk. His face was hidden in his hand. And he was peeking through his fingers—right at her test.

Michelle gulped.

Jeff Farrington was a nice guy. He was her pal! Could he really be *cheating?*

Chapter

3

♥ *Now* what do I do? Michelle wondered.

She felt a flash of anger. I should raise my hand and tell Mrs. Yoshida right now! she thought.

She started to raise her hand. Then stopped.

What if Jeff wasn't cheating?

Maybe he was just staring at how messy her paper was. Maybe he was daydreaming about what his mom packed for lunch!

Besides, she didn't want to get Jeff in

trouble. She just wanted him to stop looking at her paper.

Michelle leaned over her desk. She
curled her arm around her test. Her face
was so close to her paper, it made her
cross-eyed to look at the numbers! Now
Jeff couldn't see it—and neither could anybody else.

"Michelle?" Mrs. Yoshida asked. "Is everything all right?"

Michelle looked up and shoved her
bangs out of her eyes. "Uh, yes," she said.
"I'm just checking my answers."

Mrs. Yoshida frowned but didn't say
anything more.

A few minutes later the teacher called
out, "Okay, class. Pencils down. Put your
papers on my desk and line up for lunch."

Michelle gave her test one more glance.
She had finished all the problems. She felt
good about her answers, too.

She laid her paper on the pile on Mrs.

Yoshida's desk. Then she went to her cubby to get her pink-and-blue lunch box.

Across the room, she spotted Jeff putting his books away. He's acting pretty normal, Michelle thought. Maybe he didn't cheat. Maybe I was only dreaming.

Stop thinking about Jeff, she told herself. Just be glad the test is over!

"How did you do?" her friend Mandy Metz whispered. Mandy's cubby was right next to Michelle's.

"Pretty good," Michelle said. "But I'm glad it's over. Fractions make my brain sore!"

That night it was Michelle's turn to set the table for dinner. Her sister Stephanie poured the drinks.

"How did you do on your test, Michelle?" her father asked. He was stirring a pot of soup on the stove.

"Better than last time, I think," Michelle said. "I did exactly what you told me. It really helped."

Danny gasped and dropped his spoon. "Quick! Someone call the newspapers!"

"Why?" Michelle asked.

"What's wrong?" Stephanie cried.

"Nothing is wrong," Danny teased. "This is a front-page story. 'Tanner Girl Takes Her Dad's Advice!'"

Michelle and Stephanie giggled.

"Cut it out, Dad," Michelle said. "We listen to you."

"Sure," Stephanie said. "At least *half* the time."

Danny grinned as he began to stir the soup again. "Then maybe I should double my advice."

"Let's see," Michelle said. She wrote on the family message board. "If we listen one half of the time to double the advice . . . what would make one half times two. That equals two halves—which equals one." Michelle underlined her answer.

"See, Dad?" she said to her father. "That means you can only give each of us one piece of advice."

Danny stared at the board. "Michelle, I don't know how it happened. But you finally know your fractions!"

That night Michelle did her math homework with extra care. She even went to bed early. She couldn't wait to go to school the next day to get back her math test!

Tomorrow was going to be the best day in fourth grade—ever!

Chapter
4

•

♥ "Don't move, Mrs. Yoshida!"

Michelle was surprised to hear Jeff yelling at their teacher. It was the next morning, and she had just walked into the classroom.

Jeff was at the blackboard with a big piece of chalk in his hand. Mrs. Yoshida stood next to her desk. She looked as stiff as a statue. What was going on?

Michelle stared at the board. Jeff was drawing a picture of their teacher. It was sort of a cartoon drawing, like something in the Sunday funnies. And it looked just like Mrs. Yoshida!

"Now you can look!" Jeff told the teacher.

Mrs. Yoshida turned around. She looked surprised. "Why, Jeff! It's wonderful!" She gave his shoulders a squeeze. "I wish I never had to erase it."

"Don't!" Jeff said. "It will be worth millions when I become a famous cartoonist. Besides, it's nicer to look at a picture of you than at a bunch of math problems."

Mrs. Yoshida shook her head. "Are you trying to butter me up?" she asked.

"Why would I put butter on you?" Jeff said. He looked confused.

Mrs. Yoshida smiled. "That's something we said when I was in school," she told him. "It meant you were trying to please your teacher so that she would give you a good grade."

Jeff's eyes lit up. "Then how would you like a whole tub of butter?" he joked.

Mrs. Yoshida laughed.

The bell rang, and Michelle settled into her seat. A few last kids hurried into the classroom. Mrs. Yoshida smiled at them as she called the roll.

"Wow, Jeff," Michelle whispered. "You sure know how to butter up a teacher! She's in a great mood."

Jeff grinned. "My mom says a good laugh fixes anything."

Mrs. Yoshida snapped her roll book shut. "And now I have what you've all been waiting for," she said. She held up a stack of papers. "Math tests!"

The teacher walked between the rows of desks, handing back the corrected tests.

Some kids shouted "Yes!" when they saw their grades. A few kids just groaned.

Michelle crossed her fingers and closed her eyes. Her paper landed on her desk.

Please please please please please! she thought. She opened her eyes.

She had missed only three problems. "All *right!*" Michelle cheered. That was a *lot* better than her last test!

She turned and shot a thumbs-up sign to her other best friend, Cassie Wilkins. Cassie sat across the room.

Cassie grinned back and mouthed "Hooray!"

Michelle felt as if she'd won first prize in a contest. A prize she had really earned.

"How did you do, Jeff?" Michelle asked.

Jeff shrugged. "Not too bad. But I'm still going to be a cartoonist when I grow up. I could never be a math teacher."

"Mandy could," Lee Wagner said. He and Mandy sat next to each other. Lee grinned. "I should have copied from Mandy's test," he joked. "She got a hundred."

"Wow!" Michelle exclaimed. "That's great, Mandy!"

Jeff whistled.

Mandy blushed. But she looked pleased. "I like math. It's like doing puzzles," she said.

"Will you sit next to me?" Jeff begged Mandy. "Maybe your math brains will rub off on me!"

"Yuck!" Mandy cried. "That sounds disgusting."

Michelle and her friends laughed.

I can't believe it, Michelle thought. I just got back a math test—and I'm laughing. Nothing could spoil this day!

"Michelle!" Mrs. Yoshida called. "Would you come here, please? And bring your math test with you."

Michelle slid from her seat.

Mrs. Yoshida must be pleased with my "new and improved" math grade! she

thought. Maybe she wants to congratu-
late me.

She smiled proudly as she hurried to the
teacher's desk.

But then she noticed that Mrs. Yoshida
was frowning.

That frown has my name on it, Michelle
thought. I guess she's mad because I was
talking too much. But the other kids were
talking also.

"Yes, Mrs. Yoshida?" Michelle asked.

"Would you step into the hall with me,
please?" the teacher asked.

Michelle heard everyone whispering as
she followed the teacher to the door.

"Class, please open your math books to
page seventy-three," Mrs. Yoshida said.
"Begin working on problems one through
fifteen. I'll be right back."

Mrs. Yoshida led Michelle into the hall.

Michelle was feeling very nervous. Just

standing outside in the hall made her feel guilty.

Her teacher sighed. She looked like she didn't want to say what was on her mind. Then she spoke in a gentle voice.

"Michelle, will you promise to tell me the truth about something?"

"Sure, Mrs. Yoshida," Michelle said.

Why not? I didn't talk *that* much, she thought.

The teacher gazed into Michelle's eyes. She took a deep breath.

"Michelle," she said, "did you cheat on your math test?"

Chapter 5

♥ Michelle opened her mouth—but no sound came out.

She felt the way she did when the twins jumped on her stomach. Squashed, with no air left inside.

Mrs. Yoshida—the teacher she liked so much—had just accused her of cheating!

Michelle turned bright red.

"No," she said at last. "I didn't cheat."

Mrs. Yoshida studied Michelle's face. "I was very pleased when I graded your test," she said. "But I was also a little surprised. It was *so* much better than your last test."

"That's because you're a good teacher," Michelle said. "I've also been studying really hard," she added. "And I've been getting a lot of help at home."

"It's okay to get help—when you're studying," Mrs. Yoshida said. "That's how we learn. But it's *not* okay to get help during the test."

"But I didn't!" Michelle cried. "Why don't you believe me?"

"I want to believe you," her teacher answered. "But you missed only three problems—"

"That proves it," Michelle said. "If I had cheated, I would have gotten a hundred!"

Mrs. Yoshida almost smiled at that. "But you missed the same three problems that Jeff did," she said.

"Well, don't weird things like that happen all the time?" Michelle asked. "Like in *Ripley's Believe It or Not?"*

"That's not very likely," Mrs. Yoshida replied. "Because your wrong answers were exactly the same as Jeff's wrong answers."

Michelle felt her cheeks flush red. She remembered how Jeff had been staring at her paper during the test.

Now she knew for sure—Jeff had copied her answers!

Mrs. Yoshida shook her head. "And you were erasing a lot, Michelle. That tells me you were having trouble with the problems."

"Yeah, but I—"

"You were also squirming in your seat," the teacher added. "And several times I noticed you looking at other students."

"But I was just resting my eyes!" Michelle bit her lip. That sounded pretty lame, even to her ears.

"I'll ask you again, Michelle," Mrs. Yoshida said. Her voice was kind but serious. "Did you cheat on this test?"

Michelle didn't know what to do.

Should she tell on Jeff to keep from getting in trouble herself?

Jeff was her pal. Pals didn't snitch on each other. And what would her classmates think? Would they call her a tattletale?

It felt weird to think about ratting on Jeff. Even if he was a rat himself!

Michelle stared down at her sneakers.

Then she remembered what her father always said about honesty. "Just tell the truth, and you'll be fine." Maybe this was a good time to listen to his advice.

Michelle raised her chin. She looked Mrs. Yoshida straight in the eye. "I didn't cheat," she said..

Mrs. Yoshida rubbed her forehead. "All

29

right, Michelle," she said at last. She sent Michelle back to her seat.

Whew! Michelle thought. I guess I'm off the hook!

"What's going on?" her friends Cassie and Mandy mouthed from across the room.

Michelle rolled her eyes.

"Pssst!" Jeff leaned toward her desk. "What's up?"

Michelle stared into his big brown eyes. How could he act as if nothing was wrong? He was a big cheat!

"Nothing," Michelle mumbled. She turned away and opened her math book.

The rest of the morning Michelle felt as if the teacher was watching her every move. Right before lunch, Mrs. Yoshida asked Michelle to come to her desk.

Uh-oh, Michelle thought.

Mrs. Yoshida handed Michelle a note. "Take this home to your father," the teacher said. "Have him read it and sign it. Bring it back to me tomorrow morning."

Double uh-oh!

"Yes, Mrs. Yoshida," Michelle said.

Michelle went to her cubby. The note wasn't sealed. It was just a folded piece of bright yellow paper. As soon as her teacher wasn't looking, Michelle snuck a peek.

Her heart sank at the words. The note said:

FROM THE DESK OF ANNA YOSHIDA

Dear Mr. Tanner:

I'd like to arrange an after-school conference as soon as possible. We need to discuss Michelle and her math work, especially her last test.

Any day after school this week would be fine.

Thank you.

Anna Yoshida

Michelle stuffed the note down into the very bottom of her backpack.

How would she ever explain this to her dad?

Triple uh-oh!

Chapter
6

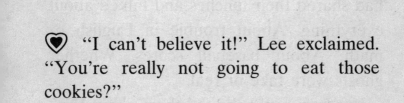 "I can't believe it!" Lee exclaimed. "You're really not going to eat those cookies?"

Michelle stared at the chocolate-chip-pecan-oatmeal cookies-with-M&M's-on-top lying in front of her.

She wasn't hungry at all. All she could think about was that awful word. It pounded in her brain: *cheat, cheat, cheat.*

"You can have them," Michelle said. She shoved the cookies across the table to Lee.

Mandy gasped at Michelle. "Are you all right?"

Michelle looked at her friends: Cassie, Mandy, and Lee. They were sitting at their favorite table in the lunchroom—the one near the window with a view of the playground.

All year long they had sat there. They had shared their lunches and talked about everything. About trouble in English or math. About baseball scores. Whether ghosts were fake or real.

But how could she tell them about this?

"Come on, Michelle," Cassie said. "We're your friends. You can tell us anything."

"Yeah, we're your friends," Lee agreed.

Michelle took a deep breath. Here goes, she thought.

"Mrs. Yoshida thinks I cheated on the math test."

Nobody said anything for a minute.

"Well, did you?" Lee blurted. His mouth was full of cookie crumbs.

"No!" Michelle cried. "How could you even think that!"

"Sorry," Lee said. He picked a blue M&M off a cookie and popped it in his mouth. "But you have been having a lot of trouble in math."

Michelle saw Cassie and Mandy exchange a worried glance.

"Do you guys think I cheated too?" she asked.

"Well . . ." Mandy twisted a strand of long dark hair around her finger. "We'd understand if you did, Michelle. We know you've been having a hard time."

"But don't worry," Cassie said. "We won't tell anybody."

Michelle couldn't believe what she was hearing. "But I didn't—"

"It's okay, Michelle," Mandy said. She looked embarrassed. "Let's not talk about it anymore. Did you see—"

"Wait!" Michelle nearly shouted. She felt hurt and angry. "I didn't cheat! Jeff did! He cheated off *my* paper! He's the one who should be in trouble."

"Wait a minute. Hold on!" Lee exclaimed. "Jeff's my buddy. I know he's not a cheater. And he would never let you get blamed for something he did. He's too nice."

Cassie looked worried. "It's not like you to try to pin the blame on somebody else, Michelle."

"But I'm not," Michelle said. "It was Jeff."

"Look," Mandy put in. "I'm not saying you cheated. But if you did, just tell Mrs. Yoshida you didn't mean to. You won't do it again. Hey—do you want to come to my house after school? Maybe I can help you study.''

"No, thanks!'' Michelle cried. Her chair screeched loudly as she stood up. "Jeff's the one who cheated, and I'm going to tell on him!''

"Wait!'' Mandy grabbed Michelle's sleeve. "Don't do that. Everybody in the whole school will call you a snitch!''

"She's right,'' Cassie said. "Once a snitch, always a snitch. Nobody will ever trust you again.''

"Besides,'' Lee added. "Why would Jeff cheat?''

"Because he's having trouble in math,'' Michelle said.

"But so are you,'' Lee pointed out. "Did *you* cheat?''

"Ooohh!'' Michelle squealed. Now they were getting her all mixed up!

She grabbed her lunch box and stomped toward the trash can.

"Wait!" Lee cried.

"Forget it!" Michelle said over her shoulder. She tossed her trash into the bin. "I'd rather be alone than with friends who think I cheat!"

Michelle spent the rest of the day feeling miserable.

Her friends thought she cheated! Why didn't they believe her?

Even worse, Jeff was acting as if nothing bad had happened. As if he wasn't the big cheat!

She didn't know what to do. She liked Jeff, and she didn't want to snitch on a friend. But it wasn't fair for her to take the blame for something he did wrong.

When the last bell rang, she hurried to catch up with Jeff. "I need to talk to you," she said.

Jeff slung a gym bag over his shoulder. "Sorry, Michelle. Got to get to soccer practice. I've missed it twice. Coach Perry might throw me off the team!"

Jeff hurried into the crowded hall. "Catch you later. On the bus tomorrow!" he called.

Michelle scowled. "I'll be waiting!" she called back.

Chapter 7

♥ Michelle took her father's green plastic kitchen timer out of her pocket. She set it to go off in twenty minutes. She placed it on her nightstand. Then she sat on her bed and picked up her homework.

"Twenty minutes," she told herself. "When the bell rings, you will get up and give Dad the note."

Her father had already seen her math test. He'd insisted on hearing all about it as soon as he got home.

"Michelle! That's wonderful!" he had

told her. "I'm so proud of you! And look." He held up the paper for Jesse and Joey. "Look how neat her columns are. That's my girl!"

Michelle knew she should have given him the teacher's note right then. But how could she?

Her dad was so happy—bragging about how great she was. She decided to wait till the time was right.

Michelle went back to her homework. She had to read the next chapter of *Little House on the Prairie,* by Laura Ingalls Wilder. Before she knew it, the bell on the timer rang.

"Phooey!" Michelle cried. She had just started another chapter.

She was having fun reading. And giving her dad the note from Mrs. Yoshida would *not* be fun.

One more chapter, she told herself. Then I will *really* give Dad the note.

She made the next chapter last as long as she could. Finally she finished the very last line of the very last paragraph.

Go on, Michelle, she told herself. Get it over with! You'll feel a whole lot better . . . maybe.

She put down her book and shuffled into the hall. She stopped halfway down the stairs.

She could hear her father humming loudly in the kitchen. He sounded so happy. And giving him the note would ruin his mood for sure.

"After supper," Michelle muttered. She scooted back to her room and plopped down on her bed. "After all," she told her favorite teddy bear, "I can't make Dad mad while he's cooking. He might burn everyone's dinner!"

A few minutes later D.J. stuck her head in the room. "Dad says you get to skip setting the table tonight. You must have really aced that math test."

"Well, sort of," Michelle said.

"Good going!" D.J. slapped her a high five. "Dad says don't come down till he calls you. Okay?"

"Okay," Michelle said. Her dad had better stop being so nice to her, she thought. Or she'd never give him the note!

Twenty minutes later Aunt Becky called Michelle to dinner. She hurried downstairs. But she stopped at the kitchen door.

All the others were standing by their places. They were staring at her. And smiling.

"Ta-da!" her dad sang out.

He'd made her favorite dinner. And he had baked her favorite chocolate cake for dessert. As a special surprise he had decorated the cake with math problems!

They were drawn in vanilla icing. There

were multiple problems, long division, and even fractions.

"Yay, Michelle!" Alex shouted.

"What did she do again, Mommy?" Nicky asked.

"She did really great on a math test," Aunt Becky explained.

"Michelle, can you help me with *my* homework after supper?" Stephanie teased.

Joey stared at the cake. "Are we sure that six times nine is fifty-four?"

"I'm sure," Michelle answered. She made herself smile. "This is great, Dad. Thanks. But . . . well, it's not like I got a hundred on my test."

"That's okay," Danny said. "It's not the grade that's important to me. It's how hard you tried. That's why I'm so proud of you."

Danny set aside the cake. Everyone sat down and began to eat their dinner.

Michelle had a hard time eating. She almost choked on her food. She *had* tried hard on her test. She had earned her grade fair and square. This should have been one of the best nights of fourth grade.

But one thing spoiled it all.

The note hidden at the bottom of her backpack.

That night Michelle and Stephanie were brushing their teeth, getting ready for bed. Michelle stared at her big sister. She was pretty nice, as sisters went.

And Stephanie was in middle school. She had lots of experience with problems like this. Maybe she could help Michelle figure out what to do.

"Stephanie," Michelle said, "can I ask you a question?"

Stephanie rinsed her mouth. "You just did."

"Really, Steph," Michelle said. "I, uh—" She stopped.

"What's up, Michelle?" Stephanie looked really interested.

"Well . . . I have this friend," Michelle said. "And, uh, she's got a problem."

"A friend, huh?" Stephanie started brushing her long blond hair. "What's her problem?"

"Well, she took this math test. She worked really hard on it. Then this guy she thought was a friend cheated off her paper. But the teacher thinks *she's* the one who cheated."

Stephanie frowned. "Why doesn't she just tell the teacher the truth?"

"I did!" Michelle cried. "Ooops!" She clapped her hands over her mouth. In the mirror she saw her face turn red.

Stephanie folded her arms. "Does your friend's name happen to be . . . *Michelle?*"

Michelle sighed. "You guessed it. I'm the one in trouble."

"So who's the real cheater?" Stephanie

asked. They walked into the bedroom they shared.

"His name is Jeff Farrington. I helped him with his math homework the other day."

"What do you mean by help?" Stephanie asked.

"I mean, I let him see my homework paper," Michelle said.

"See?" Stephanie repeated. "Or *copy?"*

"Well, he sort of copied," Michelle said. "He said he didn't have time to do it at home."

Stephanie pulled back the covers on her bed. "You shouldn't let him copy your homework. That's cheating too."

"It is?" Michelle asked.

"Think about it," Stephanie said. "He copies *your* work, then turns it in with *his* name on it? That's not cool."

"You're right," Michelle mumbled. "But I wanted him to like me. And he said

47

we were friends. I thought I was helping him."

"You were helping him," Stephanie said as she climbed into bed. "Helping him cheat!"

"I guess," Michelle said. "And then he cheated off my math test, too. It's awful, Steph! The teacher thinks *I* cheated. And so do my friends."

"Did you cheat, Michelle?" Stephanie asked.

"No way!" Michelle cried.

"Okay, okay, I believe you!" Stephanie turned out the light.

"What should I do?" Michelle asked. "How do I prove to Mrs. Yoshida that I'm not a cheater?"

"Tell her Jeff did it."

"You mean snitch on him?"

"Hey," Stephanie said. "Would you call it snitching if you turned in a bank robber?"

"Nope."

"Well, Jeff's a thief too. He stole your hard work."

Michelle thought about that. In the darkness she pictured Jeff in a bank robber's costume. But instead of stuffing a bag with money, he was stuffing it with fractions!

Michelle giggled. Then she grew serious.

"But what if Mrs. Yoshida doesn't believe me?" Michelle said. "What if she thinks I'm just trying to get Jeff in trouble? She really likes him."

"Teacher's pet, huh?" Stephanie yawned. "Then the only thing to do is talk to Jeff. Get him to tell the teacher that he's the one who cheated."

Michelle sighed. "Things were a lot easier when I was a little kid."

"Just wait till you get to middle school!" Stephanie said.

Michelle snuggled into the covers. It felt

good to have a big sister to tell her problems to. But there was still one problem she hadn't told Stephanie about.

The note from Mrs. Yoshida.

Michelle tossed and turned. She wondered if Jeff the rat was having trouble falling asleep. She hoped so!

Michelle made herself a promise. She'd give her dad the note first thing in the morning. Then she would talk to Jeff on the bus.

And then she hoped that Jeff would do the right thing.

Because all he had to do was tell the truth—and get her out of this awful mess!

Chapter
8

♥ The next morning Michelle leaped out of bed early. She dressed in a red T-shirt, navy leggings, and white high-top sneakers.

Then she took the note out of her back-pack and smoothed out the wrinkles. "Just do it!" she told herself. She ran downstairs to show the note to her dad.

Nikki and Alex were hiding under the kitchen table. Uncle Jesse crawled underneath it. He was trying to talk them into eating their breakfast. The twins were pretending to be dogs. They wanted to eat on the floor with Comet.

D.J. was nibbling toast while she read a book for college. She was always studying. "You're up early," she said to Michelle.

"Where's Dad?" Michelle asked.

"Gone," D.J. said. She turned the page and glanced up. "To work. You know, that place he goes every morning to earn money?"

"But it's still early!"

D.J. carried her plate and glass to the sink. "He and Aunt Becky had to get to the studio extra early this morning. Some kind of special meeting."

Michelle groaned. She couldn't believe it! Now there was no way she could get him to sign the note.

D.J. saw that Michelle was upset. "Don't worry, Michelle," she said. "Uncle Jesse will make sure you get to school okay. Right, Uncle Jess?"

They heard something bonk the underside of the table.

"Ow!" Uncle Jesse crawled out and stood up, rubbing his head. "Right. Do you want me to drive you girls to school?"

D.J. shook her head. "Nope, I've got a ride."

Michelle plopped down at the table. "I have to ride the bus," she said. She reached for a glass of fresh-squeezed orange juice.

Joey came in and poured himself a cup of coffee. "Morning, everybody!"

"Joey," Michelle said. "I need to tell a teacher I couldn't do what she asked me to. Do you know any good excuses?"

Joey rubbed his chin. " 'I lost it'?"

Uncle Jesse lifted one of the twins. "How about 'My dog ate it'?"

D.J. grabbed her books. "How about 'It was in my pocket and my dad accidentally washed it'?"

Stephanie stumbled into the kitchen. "How about 'I overslept'?" she said.

"And then there's my personal favorite," Joey added.

"What?" Michelle asked.

" 'I forgot,' " Joey said.

"Well, try to remember," Jesse told him. "The kid needs help."

Joey laughed. "No, no, no. That *is* the excuse—'I forgot!' It works every time!"

After breakfast Michelle climbed on the school bus. She hurried toward the back. That's where Jeff usually sat. But Jeff wasn't there. He was nowhere on the bus!

Had he missed it? Or was he avoiding her?

Was the rat a chicken, too?

Michelle was one of the first kids to arrive in her classroom. She sat at her desk. The bell hadn't even rung yet.

Mrs. Yoshida came in and headed straight for Michelle. "Michelle," Mrs. Yoshida said, "may I have the note from your father, please?"

Quick! Michelle told herself. Pick an excuse!

"Uh—uh—I forgot," she squeaked.

Mrs. Yoshida crossed her arms and frowned. "Michelle," she said quietly, "will you stay after school this after-noon?"

Joey's excuse had bombed. Michelle blushed. "Yes, Mrs. Yoshida."

The bell rang. Michelle glanced across the aisle. Jeff wasn't at his desk. Maybe he felt so rotten about cheating that he was home with a stomachache!

But a few minutes later he ran into the classroom. He gave Mrs. Yoshida a tardy note, then hurried to his seat. His face was red, and he was breathing hard.

"Missed the bus," he whispered to Michelle. "Had to run all the way."

He smiled at her as if nothing was wrong.

Just wait till recess, Jeff Farrington, Michelle thought. Just you wait!

Chapter 9

♥ At recess Jeff asked Michelle to join in a game of softball. She couldn't talk to him. Not in front of everybody.

Michelle grabbed a bat and walked up to home plate. Jeff stood on the pitcher's mound. Cassie was on first base. Mandy was on second. And Lee watched her from third.

"Heads up, everybody!" Jeff shouted to his teammates. "Michelle's a great batter. Watch the way she swings and *copy* her!"

Copy me! Michelle thought. *Grrrrr!* That really made her mad!

Jeff wound up and threw the pitch. *WHAM!*

Michelle hit the ball so hard it shot deep into the outfield.

Jeff grinned as he watched the ball fly toward the school yard fence. "What did I tell you! She's awesome!"

Michelle scowled as she trotted around the bases.

She didn't speak to Cassie on first base, Mandy on second, or Lee on third. She was still angry with them for not believing that she hadn't cheated.

When it was time to go in, she caught Jeff by the arm.

"Wait up, Jeff. I need to talk to you."

Jeff smacked the softball into his leather glove. "Sure, Michelle. Man, you are one amazing batter."

"Forget it, Jeff," Michelle said. "You can't butter me up like you do the teacher."

Jeff looked surprised. "But I mean it! You're a *great* softball player. And a great pal!"

"But you're not," Michelle blurted. "What about the math test?"

"Math test?"

"You *know* what I'm talking about, Jeff," Michelle said. "First you talked me into letting you copy my math home-work—"

"But Michelle. You *said* I could!"

"I know. But I shouldn't have."

"Don't worry about it," Jeff said. "Everybody does it sometimes."

"Well, I don't. Not anymore. It's cheating."

"Cheating!" Jeff exclaimed. "You were only helping me with homework. It's not like it was a test or anything."

Michelle folded her arms. "And what about the test?"

"Huh?" Jeff said. "What—what do you mean?"

"Come on, Jeff, the math test!" Michelle looked him square in the eye. "You cheated off my paper. Didn't you?"

Jeff stared down at his softball glove. "I don't like being called a cheater," he said in a low voice.

Michelle gulped. But she didn't give in. "Did you copy my paper or didn't you?"

Jeff glanced around him. Then he drew Michelle off to the side. "Okay, look. I was having trouble on the test. But I knew you'd been working hard on your math lately. So I just, sort of . . . well, I borrowed some of your answers."

"Borrowed?" Michelle cried. "When were you planning to give them back?"

Jeff grinned. "Hey, that's pretty funny."

Michelle sighed. "I'm not trying to be funny. How could you do it, Jeff?"

Jeff kicked at the ground. "Aw, shoot. Things have been rough at my house, Michelle. You know I've been looking after my little brothers a lot."

"Yeah, so?"

"So, I didn't tell you why." Jeff's shoulders slumped. "I think my parents are going to get a divorce. My mom's gone back to work, and I have to help out a lot at home. Things are pretty crazy in my house right now. I hardly ever have time for schoolwork."

"Oh." Michelle wasn't sure what to say. "I'm sorry."

Jeff shrugged. "That's okay."

"But you still shouldn't have cheated off my paper!"

"I know," Jeff agreed. "But it was an emergency! The last thing my mom needs is for me to bring home a bunch of bad grades. She's got enough to worry about."

"But Jeff—"

"Please don't snitch on me, Michelle," Jeff begged. "It would really upset my mom. Come on, it'll be our secret."

"But—" Michelle began.

"I promise I won't do it again," Jeff said. "Who's it hurting, anyway?"

"Time to go in, kids!" Mrs. Yoshida clapped as she called to Michelle, Jeff, and a few other stragglers.

Jeff hurried inside.

Who's it hurting? Michelle asked herself. *Me!*

She walked slowly toward the door. She felt sorry for Jeff because he had problems. But that didn't change how she felt about his cheating.

She hadn't even told him that Mrs. Yoshida thought she had cheated on the test.

She wondered if it would make any difference to him.

Michelle sighed. Things couldn't possibly get any worse.

Michelle stayed behind when the bell rang that afternoon. She watched the other kids scramble out of the classroom. Mandy gave her a worried smile.

"Call me," Cassie said.

Michelle waved good-bye. Then she saw something awful through the tiny glass window in the door: her father's face.

And he did *not* look happy.

Chapter
10

♥ "Hello, Michelle," Danny said.

Michelle tried to smile. "Uh, hi, Dad!"

"Mrs. Yoshida called. She asked me to come by after school," he said. "It seems you forgot to give me something. A note, maybe?"

"I was going to!" Michelle cried. "But it never seemed like the right time."

"Is now a good time?"

"I guess so." Michelle pulled the note from her backpack and gave it to her father.

He read it without saying a word.

"Hello, Mr. Tanner," Mrs. Yoshida called from her desk. "Could we talk alone for a minute?"

"Sure," Danny answered. "I think that's a good idea."

Michelle sat at her desk while her father and her teacher talked quietly at the front of the room. She tried to read *Little House on the Prairie.* But the words ran together on the pages.

At last her teacher asked her to join them.

"Michelle, you've always been a good student," Mrs. Yoshida said. "You always try hard. And you work well with others."

"Thank you," Michelle said.

Mrs. Yoshida shifted in her seat. "That's why I'm so worried about this test."

"Mrs. Yoshida, I must say that Michelle has been working very hard on her math,"

Danny said. "We've all been helping her. Maybe she's really doing better."

"I'd like to believe that," Mrs. Yoshida said. "It's just those matching wrong answers that bother me."

Danny turned to Michelle. "Honey? Do you have something to say?"

Michelle swallowed. "All I can say is I didn't cheat on the test."

"All right, Michelle. We'll leave it at that." Mrs. Yoshida stood up and held out her hand. "Thank you for stopping by, Mr. Tanner."

"It was no problem," Danny said. "But Michelle and I will have a long talk about this at home."

The teacher smiled. "Great. Good-bye now."

Danny dropped Michelle off at home, but then he had to go back to work. "We'll talk about this tonight," he told Michelle.

Michelle nodded slowly. She watched him drive away.

"I can't wait," she mumbled.

It was almost bedtime. Michelle watched as Stephanie carried an armful of magazines toward the bathroom.

"If I'm not out of my bubble bath in an hour, send in a search party!" Stephanie called.

Danny stopped in the doorway. "That should give Michelle and me plenty of time for Dad Talk Number 247."

"Let's see. Is that the one about staying out late on a school night . . . ?" Stephanie said as she wandered down the hall.

"Hmmm," Danny said. "Maybe I should put my talks on the computer. Then you girls could punch in a code and get my advice anytime." Danny sat down on Michelle's bed.

"I'm sorry, Dad," Michelle said before

he could speak. "I guess you're pretty mad at me."

Danny sighed. "Not exactly, Michelle. I'm mostly upset that you didn't give me the note."

"I guess I was scared," Michelle told him.

"Michelle, you should never be afraid to tell me anything," Danny said. "Why be afraid if you didn't cheat?"

"I was afraid you wouldn't believe me."

Danny sighed. "Maybe it's my fault. Making you worry too much about getting a good grade."

"No! I just wanted to do well. I didn't cheat," Michelle insisted. "You do believe me—don't you?"

Danny was thoughtful. "Well, if you say you didn't cheat . . ."

He gave her a kiss on the cheek. Then he tucked her in and left the room.

Michelle buried her face in her pillow

and burst into tears. He *wanted* to believe her. But she saw the look in her father's eyes. He wasn't really sure!

My own father, Michelle thought. He's worried that I really did cheat!

There has to be a way to prove I didn't do it. There *has* to be!

Chapter

11

♥ "Okay, class, put away your math books," Mrs. Yoshida said the next morning. "And take out one clean sheet of paper."

"Uh-oh . . ." Jeff whispered to Michelle. "I've got a bad feeling about this."

"We're going to have a little pop quiz," the teacher announced. She turned and began to write problems on the board.

"Nooo!" some of the kids moaned.

"Yay!" Michelle cried.

"Huh?" Jeff stared at Michelle with his mouth hanging open.

"Are you crazy?" Lee whispered from his desk.

Michelle jumped up from her seat. She had just come up with a terrific idea. A way to prove she wasn't a cheater!

"Hey, where are you going?" Jeff asked.

Michelle grinned. "Wait and see," she said.

Michelle hurried to the teacher's desk. "Mrs. Yoshida?"

The teacher turned around. "Yes?"

"May I move to that empty seat next to the window for the test?" Michelle asked.

Mrs. Yoshida frowned. "I think it's best if you sit in your own seat."

"Please!" Michelle begged. "I want to prove to you I don't cheat!"

Mrs. Yoshida stared hard at Michelle. "All right," she said at last.

"Thanks!" Michelle carried her paper

and pencil to the desk by the window and sat down.

"Okay, class," Mrs. Yoshida called out. "You may begin."

Michelle grabbed her pencil and pounced on the test. It was tough. As tough as the last one.

But she took each problem one by one. She kept her columns neat. And she kept her eyes on her own paper.

At last she was finished. She stopped and stretched. Then she glanced—very quickly—at Jeff.

He seemed to be having trouble. Erasing a lot. His usual cheery smile was flipped over into a frown. Michelle felt bad for him. She knew what it was like to struggle on a test. Poor Jeff!

Michelle went back to her own test. Very carefully she double checked each problem.

"Time's up," Mrs. Yoshida called.

Michelle wrote her name in the upper-right-hand corner of her paper. Then she turned in her paper and went back to her seat.

She glanced at Jeff. He gave her a weak smile. But he looked a little green.

At lunchtime Mrs. Yoshida sent the class to the cafeteria. But she asked Michelle and Jeff to wait.

Jeff shot Michelle a nervous look. They sat down near the teacher's desk.

"I've had a chance to grade the pop quiz," the teacher said. "Michelle—I'm quite surprised by your test."

Uh-oh, Michelle thought. Had she messed up?

Mrs. Yoshida grinned and handed Michelle her paper. "Don't worry! You missed only one problem. Congratulations!"

Michelle stared at her paper. She

couldn't believe it! Her dad was going to be so proud!

"Now yours, Jeff," the teacher said. "You left nearly half the test blank. And what are all these scratches and eraser marks?"

Jeff tried to make a joke. "Uh, fleas?"

Mrs. Yoshida sighed. "Jeff, I thought Michelle cheated off your last math test."

Jeff stuffed his hands in the pockets of his jeans. He didn't say a word.

"You both had three wrong answers on that test," the teacher added. "Three wrong answers that matched exactly. What do you say about that, Jeff?"

"A weird accident?" he mumbled.

"Jeff," Mrs. Yoshida said. She waited till he looked up at her. "Did you cheat off Michelle's paper on the last test?"

Michelle held her breath.

Jeff smiled as if he were about to make a joke. But then he looked at Michelle and his smile faded. His face turned red, and he stared at the floor.

"Yeah . . ." His voice was so soft Michelle could hardly hear him. "I'm the one who cheated. Not Michelle."

Michelle let out a big sigh. She was off the hook!

Mrs. Yoshida's voice was stern. "How could you let Michelle take the blame for something you did?"

"I didn't mean to!" Jeff exclaimed. "I never cheated before. Honest! I didn't think one test was that big a deal."

Then Jeff told Mrs. Yoshida everything. He told her about his problems at home. About falling behind in his work.

"I thought it would be okay to cheat a little—as long as I didn't get caught," he said. "But then Lee told me Michelle got in big trouble for it."

Jeff squirmed in his seat. "I didn't know what to do! I was afraid to tell the truth."

He glanced at Michelle. "I didn't mean to hurt Michelle."

"But don't you see?" Mrs. Yoshida said gently. "Your cheating hurt two people. Michelle—and someone else."

Jeff looked puzzled. "Who?"

"You," the teacher said.

Jeff stared at the floor and nodded. Mrs. Yoshida turned to Michelle. "You knew Jeff cheated off your paper. Why didn't you speak up and tell me?"

"I didn't want to be a tattletale," Michelle said. "And I didn't want the other kids to call me a snitch."

"I see." Mrs. Yoshida stood up. "Jeff, I think you owe Michelle an apology."

Jeff kept his eyes on the floor. "Sorry, Michelle."

Michelle was glad Jeff had told the truth. But she felt bad for him, too. He looked so miserable.

"Can I say something else?" Michelle

asked. "I gave Jeff my homework to copy. I know now that was cheating too."

"You're right," Mrs. Yoshida said. "It's okay to study together and give each other help. But when you sign your name to your paper, you're saying 'this is my work.' "

Mrs. Yoshida leaned forward and chuckled. "You know, homework is not a chore that teachers invented to ruin your afternoons. Homework helps me know if I'm doing a good job of teaching. It helps me know which student needs more help."

"I guess it's me," Jeff said.

The teacher smiled. "That's what I'm here for!"

Mrs. Yoshida stood up and walked Michelle to the door. "Michelle, I'm sorry I didn't believe you. Will you forgive me?"

"Sure," Michelle said. She gave her teacher a quick hug. "Thanks, Mrs. Yoshida."

"Please tell your father I'll call to tell

him how things turned out," the teacher added.

Michelle nodded. Then she turned to wave good-bye to Jeff.

But he wouldn't look at her.

Oh, no, Michelle thought. Now he's mad at me for getting him into trouble! She frowned.

I guess we aren't pals anymore, she thought.

Chapter

12

♥ "Forget about a special dinner," Danny Tanner said.

It was later that day. Everyone was gathered in the living room. Danny held up Michelle's math test for everyone to see.

"Michelle, your grade on this quiz deserves chocolate cake *and* ice cream sundaes!" he told her.

"Great, Dad!" Michelle giggled. "But what will you do if I ever get a hundred on a test?"

"Let's see." Danny pretended to think hard. "How about a trip to Disneyland?"

"Wait a minute," Stephanie said. "Let me get this down in writing!"

"Right!" D.J. agreed with a laugh. "I've got a big history test coming up. If I do well, maybe I could win a trip to Hawaii!"

Everyone laughed. Danny gave Michelle a big hug. "Mrs. Yoshida called me this afternoon and explained everything," he said. "I'm proud of you, sweetheart. And I'm sorry I didn't believe you the first time. Forgive me?"

"Sure," Michelle said.

"There's just one thing I don't understand," Danny went on. "Why didn't you tell me what Jeff did in the first place?"

"I didn't want to be a snitch," Michelle said. "But I guess it was wrong not to tell you the whole truth. Sorry, Dad."

"That's okay," Danny said. He hugged her again.

Riiiing!

Joey answered the phone. "Michelle, it's for you," he said.

Michelle hurried to the phone. "Hello?"

"Hi, Michelle. It's Cassie."

"Oh. Hi."

"Michelle, I heard all about how Jeff really did cheat off your test."

Michelle was surprised. "How did you find out?"

"Jeff told Lee. And Lee told me," Cassie explained. "I'm sorry I didn't believe you in the first place. Forgive me?"

Suddenly Michelle felt great. "Sure." They talked a few more minutes before saying good-bye.

Michelle hung up and went back to sit on the sofa. A moment later the phone rang again.

This time Becky answered. "Michelle, it's for you again," she said.

Michelle picked up the phone. "Hello?"

"Hi, Michelle. It's me—Mandy."

"Hi, Mandy."

"I heard about Jeff cheating off your test!"

"Who told you?" Michelle asked.

"Jeff told Lee. And Lee told Cassie. And Cassie told me."

Mandy was quiet for a minute. Then she blurted, "Please don't be mad at me! I'm sorry I didn't believe you about the cheating. I'll always believe you from now on. Are we still friends?"

Michelle felt double great! "Sure," she said. They chatted for a few minutes, then Michelle hung up.

Michelle started to head toward the sofa. But she stopped when the phone rang one more time.

Uncle Jesse shook his head and grinned.

"Why don't you answer it, Michelle. I have a feeling it's for you."

Michelle giggled and went to answer the phone. "Hello?"

"Hi, Michelle. It's Lee."

Michelle grinned. "Okay, okay. I forgive you."

"Huh?" Lee said. "For what?"

"Aren't you calling to say you're sorry?"

"Sorry about what?"

"That you thought I was a cheater?"

Lee laughed. "No, no. I forgot all about that. I was just calling to see if my mom could have your dad's recipe for those cookies you brought to school the other day. The ones with the M&M's?"

"Forget it, Lee—it's a family secret! Bye!"

Just then the doorbell rang. "I'll get that!" D.J. cried. "Michelle, it's for you."

Michelle rolled her eyes. This was getting ridiculous! She leaped up from the sofa.

Jeff Farrington stood in the doorway. "Uh, hi, Michelle," he said.

"Hi, Jeff," Michelle said.

"Can I come in for a minute?" he asked.

"Sure. Come on in." Michelle introduced Jeff to everyone in her family.

"Wow," Jeff said. "You weren't kidding. You do have a full house."

The twins raced over to him. Nicky tried to swing on Jeff's arm. Alex drove his new toy car right up Jeff's leg. Jeff just laughed.

"You must be used to this because of your little brothers," Michelle said.

"You're right," Jeff agreed. "I really like little kids."

"Do you?" Michelle's dad asked. Danny folded his arms and squinted at Jeff. He

84

looked as if he was planning to give Jeff one of his famous talks!

"Dad!" Michelle ran over and whispered in his ear. "Don't say anything! Everything's okay now."

"Oh, all right," Danny whispered back. "But don't let him copy your homework. Or any of my recipes!"

"Don't worry!" Michelle said with a giggle.

She hurried over to rescue Jeff from the twins.

"Um, Michelle," Jeff said. "Could I talk to you alone?"

Michelle frowned at the crowded living room. It wasn't so easy to be alone in her house.

"Use our room," Stephanie said. "I'll stay down here."

"Thanks, Steph," Michelle said. She led Jeff up to the room she shared with Stephanie and plopped onto the bed. Jeff sat on the desk chair.

Neither of them said anything for a minute.

"Uh . . . well?" Michelle said.

Jeff pulled off his red baseball cap and fiddled with the strap. "I'm sorry, Michelle," he said at last. "I never should have cheated off your math test." He stared up at her with his big brown eyes. "Can we still be friends?"

"Do you promise not to cheat off me ever again?" Michelle asked.

"Promise."

"Then I forgive you," Michelle said. "Are you mad at me for getting *you* into trouble?"

"Nah," Jeff said. "It wasn't your fault. I deserved it. And Mrs. Yoshida was really nice about everything. But—" Jeff pulled a piece of paper from his pocket. "I still got a note for my mom to sign."

"Take my advice," Michelle said. "Give it to her as soon as you get home!"

"Okay." Jeff grinned. "Do you have any advice about how to get rid of my math allergy? Maybe I could get a shot."

"No shots!" Michelle said. "I know something better. When you're sick of math—studying is the best medicine!"

❧❧❧❧❧❧❧❧❧❧❧❧❧

For information about
Mary-Kate + Ashley's Fun Club™,
the Olsen Twins' only
official fan club, write to:

Mary-Kate + Ashley's Fun Club™
859 Hollywood Way, Suite 412
Burbank, California 91505

❧❧❧❧❧❧❧❧❧❧❧❧❧

FULL HOUSE™
Michelle

Based on the Hit Warner Bros. TV Series!

Available from

A MINSTREL® BOOK

Published by Pocket Books

™ & © 1994, 1995, 1996 Warner Bros. All Rights Reserved.

1033-11

A series of novels based on your favorite character from the hit TV show!

FULL HOUSE™
Stephanie

**Available from Minstrel® Books
Published by Pocket Books**

™ & © 1993, 1994, 1995, 1996 Warner Bros. Television. All Rights Reserved. 929-12